Katie Van Camp and Lincoln Agnew

COOKIEBOT!

★★ A HARRY AND HORSIE ADVENTURE ★★

BALZER + BRAY
An Imprint of HarperCollinsPublishers

CookieBot!: A Harry and Horsie Adventure
Text copyright © 2011 by Katie Van Camp
Illustrations copyright © 2011 by Lincoln Agnew
All rights reserved. Manufactured in China.

Library of Congress Cataloging-in-Publication Data is available.
ISBN 978-0-06-197445-8

Typography by Dana Fritts
11 12 13 14 15 SCP 10 9 8 7 6 5 4 3 2 1
❖ First Edition

To our grandmothers,
who bake with equal parts sugar and love

Harry and Horsie were busy building a city out of blocks when they were interrupted by a funny sound.

GURRRRRGLE GURGLE GURRRRRGLE

"Horsie, was that you?" Harry asked. "I think we need a snack."

Horsie agreed. But they didn't want apples or cheese or carrot sticks. They wanted cookies!

There was only one problem. For some reason, Mom had placed the cookie jar way up high, too high for Harry to reach.

But as always, Horsie knew exactly what to do.

So Harry found his toolbox and got to work.
And of course Horsie helped.

"Wrench."

"Hammer."

"Spatula."

Once the sprockets were secure and the
speed control was set, Harry's invention was
finally finished.

And they called it . . .

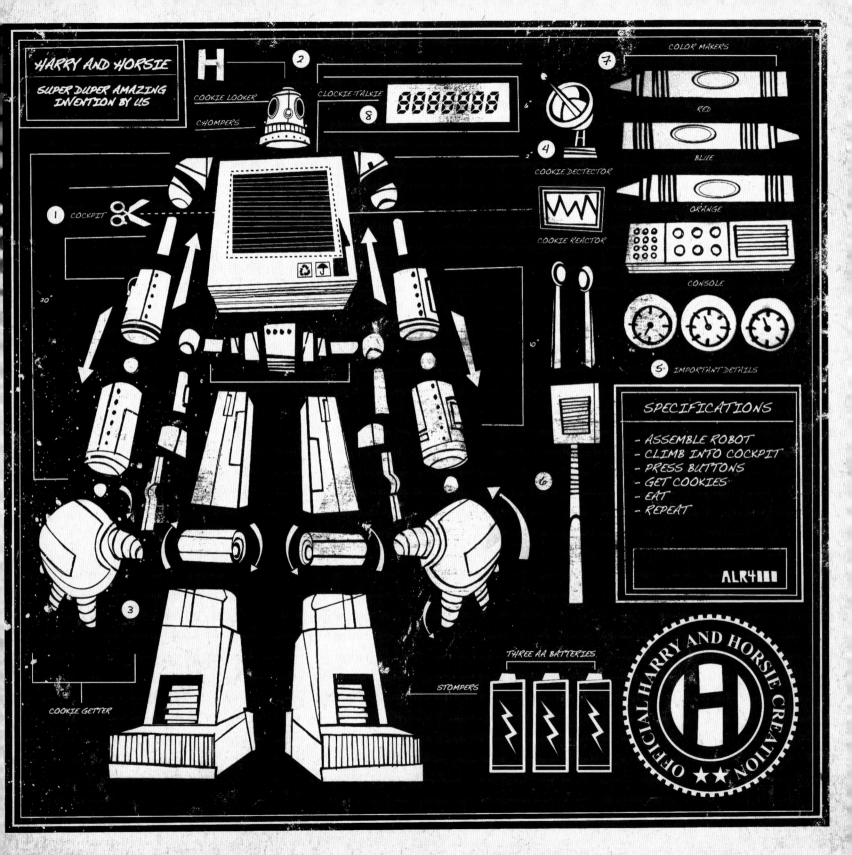

Harry pressed the ON button.
CLANK-CLANK! ZOOP-ZOOP! ZZZZZZ!
"All right! Time to get us some cookies!"

He used the controls to maneuver CookieBot's arm in through the kitchen window.
"Easy does it," Harry whispered.

CookieBot took the lid off the cookie jar. Then he grabbed a chocolate chip cookie and handed it to Horsie.

"One for you—now one for me!"

But CookieBot had other ideas. He picked up the jar and emptied it into his mouth.

"Uh-oh," Harry cried. "He's out of control!"

But before Horsie could stop him, CookieBot charged down Fifth Avenue in search of more cookies.

Meanwhile, Harry realized something terrible:
CookieBot had an ON switch, but there was no
way to turn him off!

If Horsie were here, he'd know exactly what to do.
But where was Horsie?

Suddenly CookieBot lurched to a stop. Harry peeked out and saw they were standing in front of a tall, tall building, and at the top of this building was the Empire Sweets Café.

CookieBot climbed toward the sugary smell. Then he yanked off the roof and started devouring every cookie in sight.

If we don't stop him soon, Harry thought, there won't be a single cookie left in the whole city—and it will be all my fault!

Just then Harry heard something. . . .

Brrrrrrr

BRRRRRRRRR

Could it be?

HORSIE!

Horsie swooped down right in front of CookieBot. Then he dropped the bait: an enormous rainbow sugar cookie.

CookieBot lunged for the tempting treat.

"Come on, CookieBot," Harry called. "I know you want that yummy cookie!"

Then Horsie started to fly around
and around and around.
ZOOOOM!

And CookieBot's head spun
around and around and around.
ZOOOOM!

Faster and faster and faster . . .
ZOOOOM!

Until CookieBot was so dizzy he
fell over—

BOOM!

"SUGAR CRASH!!"

Cookie crumbs rained down over the city, and sprinkles sparkled in the sky.

"You did it!" Harry shouted to his friend.

Horsie knew exactly what to do next. He took Harry home—

and got him a tall glass of milk!